# Once Upon a Picture

Renoir

Klee

Van Gogh

Rousseau

## Sally Swain

ALLEN & UNWIN

Once upon a picture, in 1886,
Pierre-Auguste Renoir painted 'The Umbrellas'.

Now upon a picture we might wonder
about the girl with the hoop.

What does she want to do?

Play?

**No!**

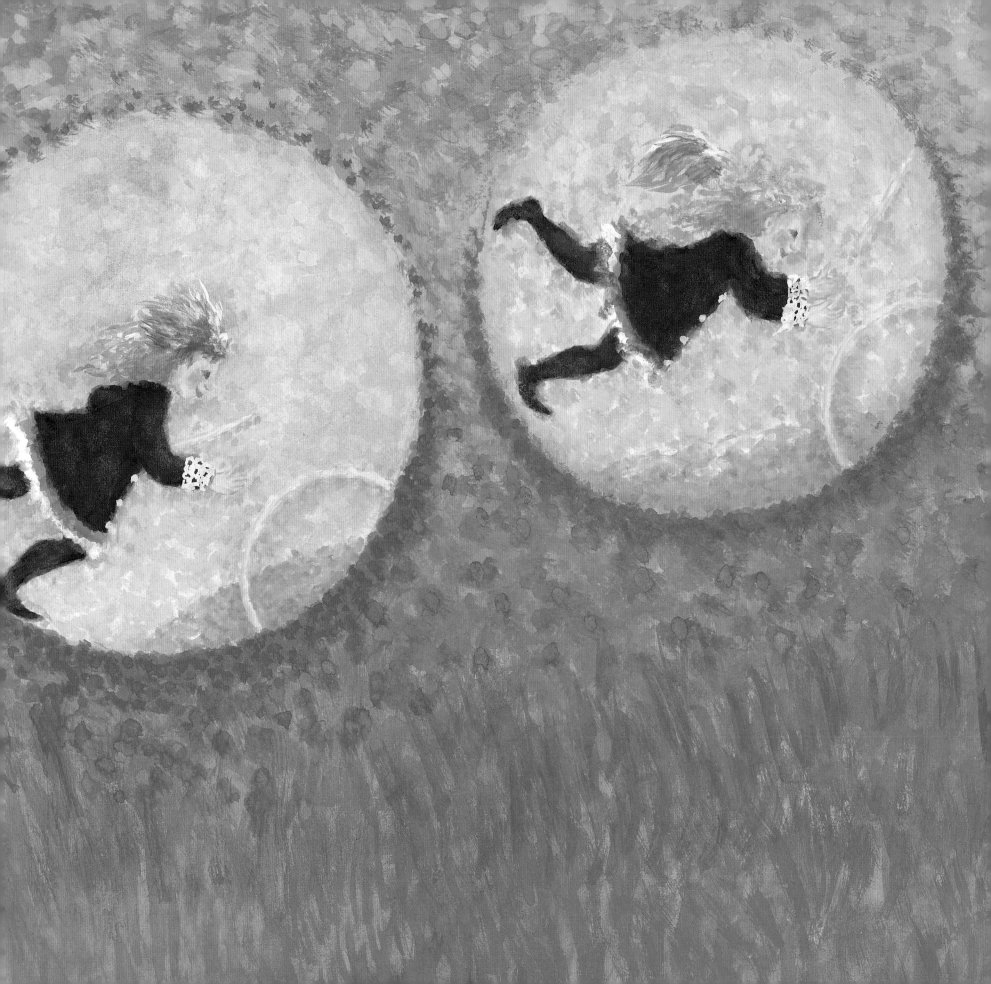

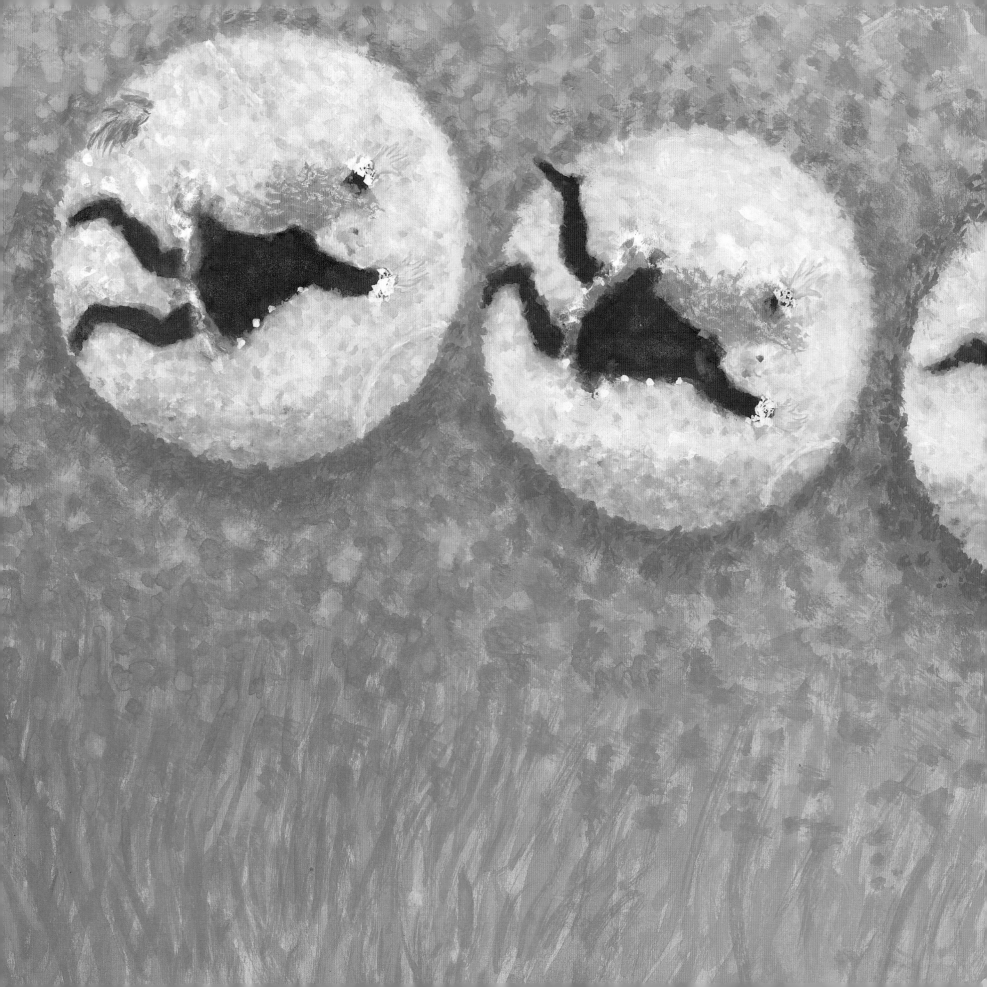

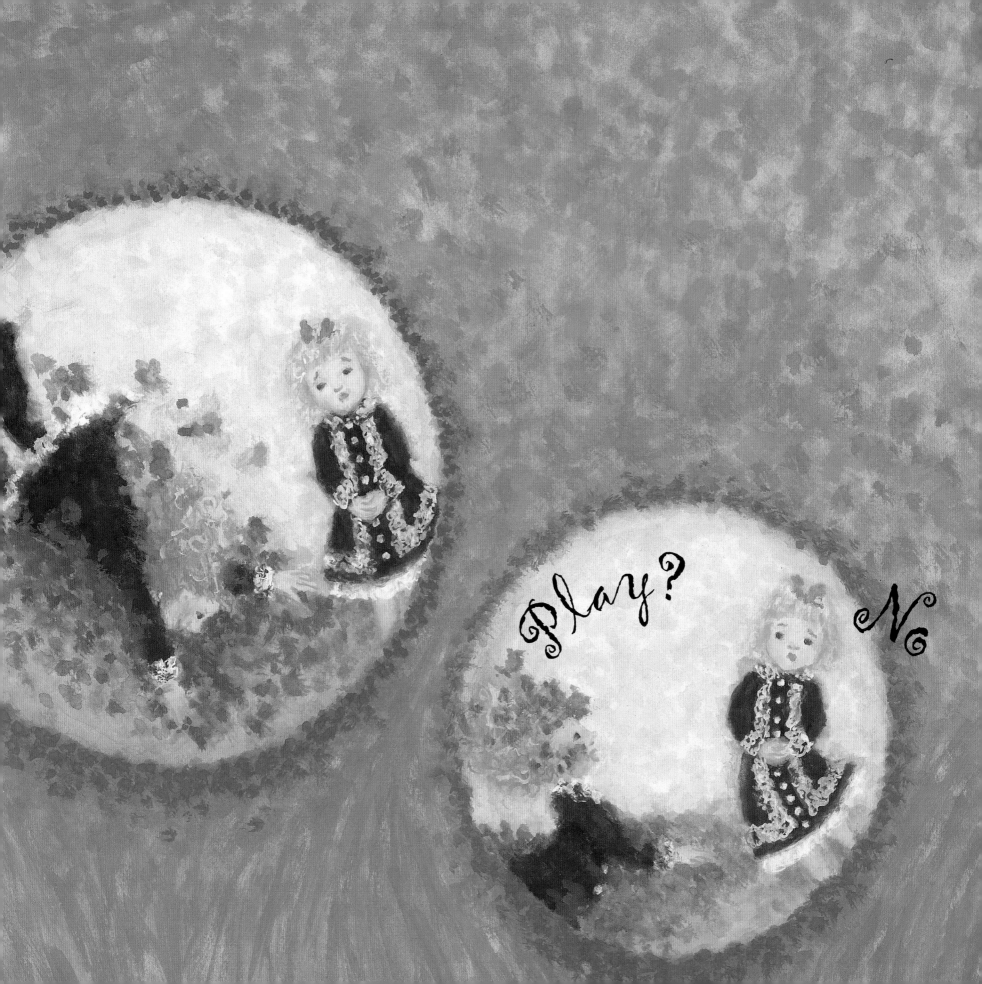

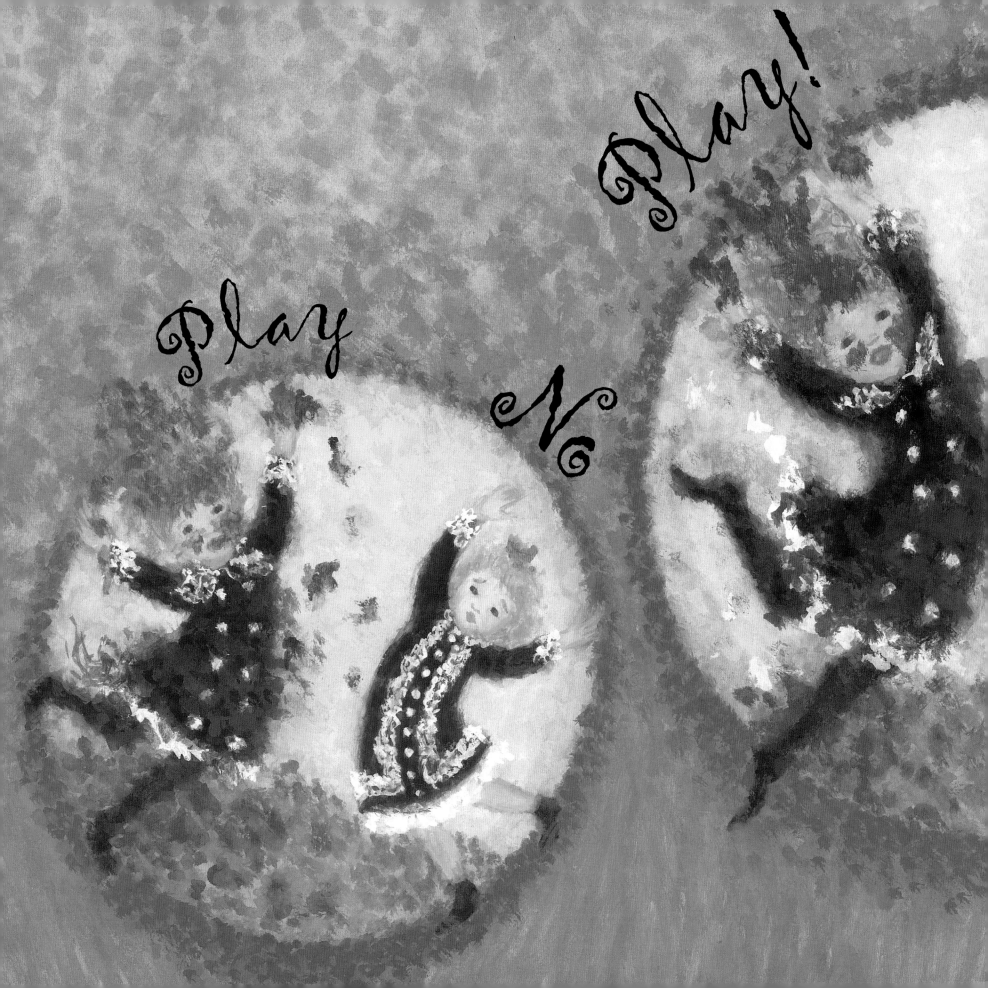

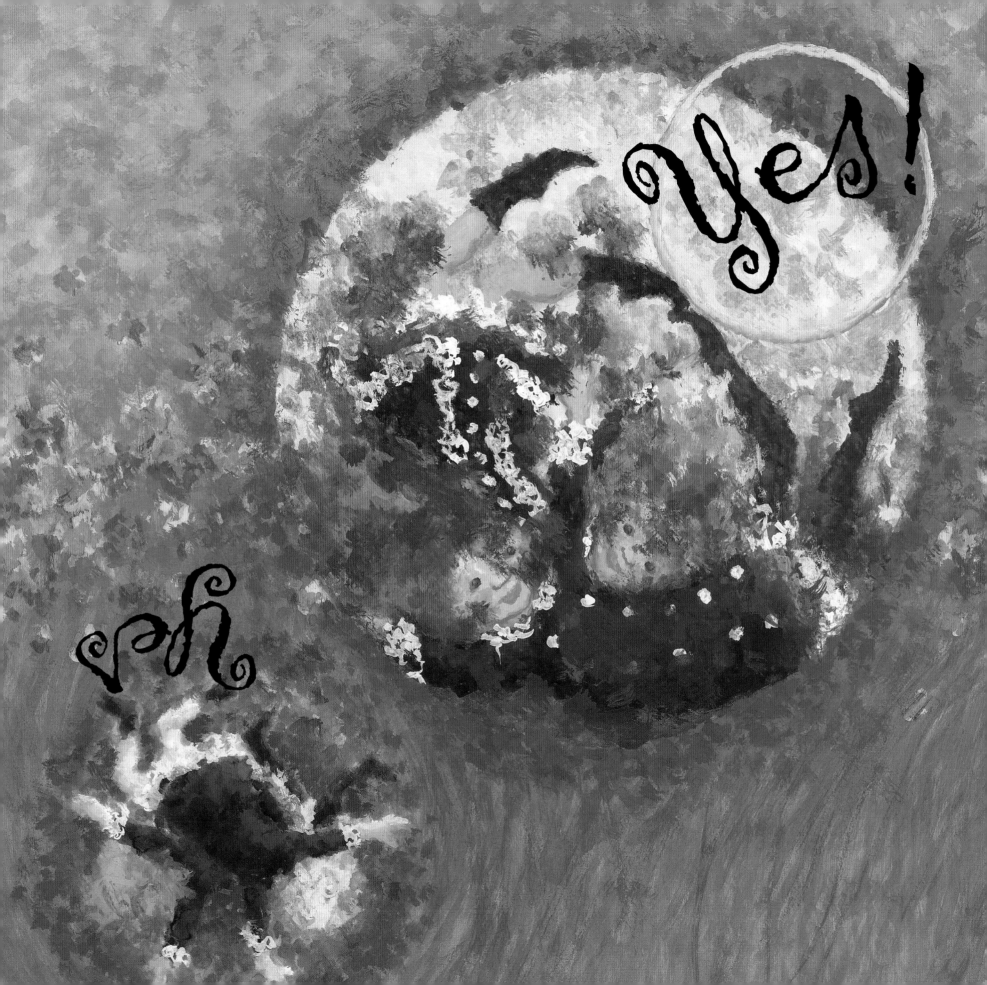

Once upon a picture, in 1922,
Paul Klee painted 'The Twittering Machine'.
Now upon a picture we might wonder
why a machine would twitter.

In the beginning there was a girl who loved a tree...

tweet

In the end the whole world twittered.

twitter

Once upon a picture, in 1889,
Vincent van Gogh painted 'The Starry Night'.
Now upon a picture we might wonder
about the moon and the stars.

Sometimes they seem very far away...

...and sometimes the moon and stars are right there beside you.

Once upon a picture, in 1891,
Henri Rousseau painted
'Tiger in a Tropical Storm (Surprised!)'.
Now upon a picture we might wonder
why the tiger is surprised.

What makes a tiger a tiger anyway?

Rousseau

Klee

Next upon a picture DISCARD YOU might wonder...

Van Gogh

Renoir